# GHOST DETECTORS

# It Creeps!

# BOOK 1

BY
## DOTTI ENDERLE

ILLUSTRATED BY
## HOWARD MCWILLIAM

magic
wagon

# visit us at www.abdopublishing.com

A special thanks to Melissa Markham — DE
For Rebecca — HM

Published by Magic Wagon, a division of the ABDO Group,
8000 West 78th Street, Edina, Minnesota 55439. Copyright
© 2010 by Abdo Consulting Group, Inc. International copyrights
reserved in all countries. All rights reserved. No part of this
book may be reproduced in any form without written permission
from the publisher.

Calico Chapter Books™ is a trademark and logo of Magic Wagon.

Printed in the United States.

Text by Dotti Enderle
Illustrations by Howard McWilliam
Edited by Stephanie Hedlund and Rochelle Baltzer
Cover and interior design by Jaime Martens

**Library of Congress Cataloging-in-Publication Data**

Enderle, Dotti, 1954-
   It creeps! / by Dotti Enderle ; illustrated by Howard
McWilliam.
      p. cm. -- (Ghost Detectors ; bk. 1)
   Summary: Ten-year-old Malcolm and his best friend Dandy,
armed with a ghost detector ordered from Beyond Belief
magazine, make a late-night trip to a haunted house, despite
warnings of Malcolm's great-grandmother.
   ISBN 978-1-60270-690-3
   [1. Ghosts--Fiction. 2. Haunted houses--Fiction. 3. Great-
grandmothers--Fiction. 4. Family life--Fiction. 5. Humorous
stories.] I. McWilliam, Howard, 1977- ill. II. Title.
   PZ7.E69645It 2009
   [Fic]--dc22
                                        2008055335

# Contents

# Con-fusion

"So are you going to help me or not?" Malcolm asked his best friend, Dandy.

"Help you do what?" Dandy asked.

Malcolm narrowed his eyes like a real scientist. "The experiment I'm about to undertake in my lab. Are you going to help me?"

Dandy, whose real name was Daniel Dee, shrugged. "What kind of experiment?"

"Fusion," Malcolm answered. He was more eager to start than to explain.

Dandy scratched his head. "Fusion? Is that a real word?"

"I don't make up words," Malcolm said. "It's real."

"Will we have to sneak your sister's blow-dryer again?" Dandy asked, grinning.

Malcolm grinned back. "Maybe." He'd say anything to get Dandy's help, except make up words.

"Count me in!"

The boys bounced down the creaky steps into Malcolm's lab. Only it was really just the basement. Malcolm had shoved most everything stored there in the corner. On a long counter he kept his chemistry set, gizmos, and gadgets. The rotten-egg odor of last week's stink bomb still hung in the air.

"Hey, Malcolm. What are we going to fu—fu—uh—fusion?"

"Money," Malcolm said. "I have an idea that I think will help the economy."

Dandy scratched his head. "What's the economy?"

Dandy was a great best friend, but for a ten-year-old, he sure didn't know much. Malcolm sighed and patiently explained, "The economy has to do with earning and spending money."

Dandy picked his nose. "Doesn't sound very scientific."

"Wait till you see what I'm going to do. You know when something costs 97¢, and you have to dig in your pocket to find three quarters, two dimes, and two pennies?"

Dandy silently counted on his fingers to double-check.

"Well, most people hate having change jingling around in their pockets, so they have to give the clerk a dollar bill. Then they get back three pennies, which means they still have change jingling around in their pockets."

"Okay," Dandy said with a blank face.

"Well, why should change be separate? Wouldn't it be easier to buy something for 97¢ if the three quarters, two dimes, and two pennies were stuck together?"

Dandy nodded his head. "Oh yeah, I get it. Like with superglue?"

"No," Malcolm said, rolling his eyes. "We'll fuse it together. Then we'll present our idea to the government and win a medal from the president."

"Cool," Dandy said, picking his nose again. "So, do you want me to sneak your sister's blow-dryer?"

"No. I want you to loan me 97¢."

"Will I get it back?" Dandy asked.

Malcolm grinned. "All in one piece."

Dandy stood with his mouth wide open as Malcolm brought out his newest prize.

"Wow! Is that your mom's curling iron?" Dandy asked.

"No," Malcolm said. "It's my latest find. And close your mouth before you swallow a fly."

Dandy snapped his mouth shut—for a moment. "Where'd you find it?"

"In the back of one of my magazines," Malcolm answered. "It's made especially for fusing metal. When I turn it on, a red-hot laser will melt the money together. Are you ready?"

Malcolm stacked the coins on the counter, biggest on the bottom. He pointed his fusion wand, then flipped the switch.

No humming. No buzzing. No whirring. Just a click.

A thin stream of white light shone down on the coins.

"I thought the laser would be red," Dandy said.

"Shhhh," Malcolm snapped, giving Dandy a warning look. "It's hot. Like a white flame."

The boys stared at the money. Dandy sniffled. "If it's that hot, wouldn't it burn a hole in the counter?"

Malcolm didn't answer, even though it was a good question. "Time's up," he finally said, clicking off the fusion wand.

Both boys inched slowly toward the table.

"Shouldn't there be smoke?" Dandy asked.

"Gosh, Dandy, don't you know anything? Lasers heat differently than fire."

They leaned forward, their noses just inches from the coins.

"Shouldn't it smell hot?" Dandy asked.

Malcolm reached his pointer finger toward the money. Slowly . . . slowly . . . slowly . . .

Dandy wiggled impatiently. "Well? Did the change . . . uh . . . change?"

Malcolm's finger touched the stack, and it came toppling down. He picked up one of the pennies. It wasn't even warm.

"What went wrong?" he muttered.

"Did you read the instructions?" Dandy asked.

"I couldn't. They were in Japanese."

Dandy picked up the fusion wand and turned it over. In tiny letters near the handle he read: *Mr. Laser Fun Flashlight—Galactic Toy Co.*

"I think I found the problem," he said, handing the flashlight to Malcolm.

Malcolm plunked himself down on an old beanbag chair. "Ripped off again! What do I do now?"

Dandy picked his nose and suggested, "Superglue?"

# Mail-Order Miracle

Malcolm dragged himself to breakfast the next morning. His pajamas were drooping and his hair was spiked from bed head.

His sister, Cocoa, and Grandma Eunice were already at the table. Cocoa was wearing blinding neon lip gloss that made her mouth look radioactive. Grandma Eunice just sat and ate her bran flakes and prunes. She was actually Malcolm's great-grandmother, and he thought she was probably older than electricity.

"Hey, coconut," Malcolm grunted.

"Mom!  Malcolm called me coconut again!" Cocoa pouted.

Mom flipped a pancake. "Malcolm, don't call your sister coconut."

"It's your fault, Mom," Cocoa whined. "If you'd given me a real name, I wouldn't have this problem."

"But sweetie," Mom said.  "Your grandmother's name was Cocoa. Aren't you honored to be named after your grandmother?"

Malcolm gave Cocoa a wicked grin. "She could have named you after a different grandmother.  How about we start calling you Eunice?"

Grandma Eunice looked up from her cereal and smiled. "That's nice."

Cocoa shot Malcolm a piercing look. "How about we call you nerd? Or do you prefer geek?"

Mom set the pancakes on the table. "I prefer quiet." She turned to Grandma Eunice, patted her shoulder, and adjusted the cereal spoon in her hand. "Can I get you something else to eat?" she asked.

Malcolm looked away. He hated the way everyone babied Grandma Eunice. They treated her more like a pet than a family member.

Grandma Eunice shook her head no, milk dripping down her chin.

Malcolm scarfed down his food and retreated to his lab to fiddle with his scientific gadgets. At midmorning he looked up through the basement window and saw feet coming up the walk. He'd know those shoes anywhere. Mail Carrier Nancy.

Malcolm dashed to the mailbox and grabbed the stack of mail. He dropped the bills, flyers, and samples on the kitchen counter. Then, he ran back to his lab, holding his magazines.

This was the time of month Malcolm loved best. His magazines always arrived on the same day, just like Christmas presents. He sorted through them.

*Junior Scientist. Weird Worlds. Beyond Belief.* They were all here. But he rarely read the articles. Instead he'd jump to the ads in the back. That's where he found the cool inventions. He especially liked the ones that advertised as, *Originally developed in a secret government lab.*

Malcolm thumbed through the back of *Beyond Belief.* Most of the ads were the same, month after month.

But a new ad caught Malcolm's eye. He practically drooled when he read it. Then, he circled it so he wouldn't forget it later.

Malcolm, who had a drawer full of batteries, leapt in the air. "Yes!"

His hands trembled as he stuffed the money into an envelope and licked it shut. He stuck on a stamp and ran to the corner mailbox. And then the waiting began.

# The Ecto-Handheld-Automatic-Heat-Sensitive-Laser-Enhanced Specter Detector

Malcolm didn't do the things that other kids did during the summer. While they were swimming and playing ball, Malcolm watched science programs and monster movies and conducted experiments in his lab. But this summer, he mostly waited . . . and waited . . . and waited.

Every day he'd sit on the front stoop, watching for Mail Carrier Nancy to approach. And every day she'd say the same thing.

"Sorry, Malcolm. No packages." He hated those words.

Then finally, after two long weeks (which felt like two eternities to Malcolm), Mail Carrier Nancy walked up, wearing a grin bigger than her face.

"I believe this is for you," she said, handing Malcolm a heavily taped box.

Malcolm wanted to jump up and hug her, but he didn't think it would be appropriate. So instead, he thanked her and ran inside the house.

He rushed past Grandma Eunice as she sat watching her favorite soap opera. "Wheeeeeee!" she sang as he sped by.

He brushed by Cocoa, nearly knocking her down. "Hey, creep!" she shouted.

But Malcolm didn't hear either one. He was already flying down the basement steps, two at a time.

He knocked some magazines and empty cups off the counter and set the box down. He wished he had X-ray vision because he couldn't wait to see inside. He quickly took a pair of scissors and sliced through the label that said *Ecto Corporation.*

When he popped up the lid, an avalanche of white foam peanuts poured to his feet. After digging through what seemed like a million of those things, including the three that stuck to his arm, Malcolm found his prize! It was wrapped in a mile of Bubble Wrap. Oh well . . . it was better than getting a broken specter detector.

Malcolm unwound and unwound and unwound until—finally—he glimpsed it. The silver metal gadget shone like a trophy. It resembled a hand drill with three small bubbles on top, one red, one green, and one gold. It was the most beautiful thing Malcolm had ever seen.

He reached in to lift it out and was surprised at how heavy it was. This was no toy. On the left side of the handle was a small door for the batteries. On the right

side was a switch. It looked easy enough. The switch was labeled Off—On—Detect.

Malcolm eyed the switch, butterflies thumping his belly. He took a deep breath and quickly flipped it on.

Nothing.

Then he remembered. *Batteries not included.*

He opened a drawer and selected two C batteries. They popped out three times before he got them installed. Then he tried the switch again. This time, he wasn't so nervous.

In the On position, the green light glowed, and the specter detector hummed. Malcolm was thrilled! He switched the gadget off and ran upstairs to the phone.

"Dandy, get over here quick. You've got to see this!"

# Lip-Synch

Malcolm stood in the front yard, waiting for Dandy. He impatiently rocked back and forth—one leg, then the other. Soon Dandy came thumping up the walk, taking his own sweet time.

"What do you want to show me?" he asked.

"It's in the lab. You gotta see it!"

When they walked into the living room, Grandma Eunice grinned at Dandy. "Hello, Alfred," she said.

Dandy looked back to make sure she wasn't talking to someone behind him. Then, he politely said, "My name is Daniel."

"That's nice," Grandma Eunice said, looking back at the TV.

The boys hurried past her and through the kitchen. Malcolm grabbed a box of cheese crackers. Seeing ketchup stains on Dandy's shirt reminded him that he'd skipped lunch.

Before they reached the basement door, Malcolm heard music blaring so loud the walls rattled below. His stomach did a somersault.

He and Dandy rushed down the steps to an unforgivable sight. There was Cocoa, bopping to the music, snapping her fingers and mouthing the words. Her neon lip gloss had peeled into crusty clumps, looking a lot like the algae in Malcolm's fish tank.

Malcolm was thankful that Cocoa wasn't really singing. Her yowling was ten times worse than her dancing. He reached back and unplugged the CD player.

"Hey, nerd!" Cocoa hollered. "I need to practice for the lip-synch contest next week. This is important."

"You can practice," Malcolm said. "But not here. Out!"

"You don't own this basement!" she said. She planted her hands so firmly on her hips, her knuckles turned white.

"This is my lab. Get out!"

Dandy sat on the bottom step, picking his nose. "What did you want to show me?"

"Not yet," Malcolm said, staring his sister down.

"I'm not leaving," Cocoa said.

"Are too."

"Am not."

"Are too."

Dandy walked over and took the box of cheese crackers from Malcolm's hand. He removed his finger from his nose, popped open the lid, and dug in.

"Ewww, your friend is gross!" Cocoa cried.

"At least his boogers end up in his mouth and not all over his lips like yours," Malcolm said.

Cocoa smacked her lips together, causing the lip gloss to curl even more. "By the way, where's my blow-dryer?"

Dandy slowly backed away, looking at the floor. Cocoa gave him a suspicious look. "Where is it?"

"Why don't you go upstairs and look for it?" Malcolm suggested.

"I'm not leaving," she said, turning around and plugging the music back in.

"Fine," Malcolm said.

He headed over to his chemistry set. Dandy followed.

Malcolm took the Bubble Wrap from the specter detector and placed it on the floor behind the counter.

"What are you doing?" Dandy asked, spraying cracker crumbs.

"Getting rid of my sister." Malcolm took a clear beaker and filled it with vinegar. Then he poured in an entire  bottle of blue food coloring. After that he grabbed a handful of white powder.

Dandy took a step back and held his nose.

"Don't worry," Malcolm said. "It's not another stink bomb. It's baking soda. When I say now, you jump."

Malcolm put the beaker on the counter and waited until Cocoa was totally engrossed in her performance. Then, he tossed the baking soda into the beaker. Blue foam boiled up.

"Ahhhhhhhh!" Malcolm screamed, slapping both hands to his face.

Cocoa clicked off the CD player in a panic. "What is it?"

Malcolm's eyes grew wide with fake fear. "Ahhhhh! I put in the wrong chemical," Malcolm shouted. "The whole basement is going to blow. Run! Now!"

Dandy turned to run, but Malcolm grabbed his shoulder and pulled him back. "Now!"

The two boys jumped high, and came down right in the middle of the Bubble Wrap. It exploded in one earsplitting bang.

Cocoa screamed and flew up the stairs, barely touching a single step. Malcolm and Dandy burst into wild laughter as Malcolm ran up and locked the basement door.

Cocoa jiggled the knob, shouting, "I won't forget this, dweeb!"

Then Malcolm turned to Dandy. "Now I can show you the greatest gadget in the world."

# Check It Out!

"Be very careful," Malcolm said. He reached in the box and removed the specter detector with the care of a surgeon.

Dandy's eyes grew wide. "You're not going to point that thing at me, are you?"

"Why would I point it at you?" Malcolm said. "You're alive."

"Yeah, and I'd like to stay that way!"

"Dandy, do you have any idea what this is?" Malcolm's chest swelled with pride.

Dandy grinned. "Did you make something out of Cocoa's blow-dryer?"

"No. It's not a blow-dryer. It's my Ecto-Handheld-Automatic-Heat-Sensitive-Laser-Enhanced Specter Detector. It's for hunting ghosts!"

"Cool!" Dandy said. "Does it work?"

Malcolm shrugged. "I don't know. I haven't tried it out yet."

"Turn it on," Dandy said, reaching for the switch.

"Wait!" Malcolm hugged the specter detector close to keep Dandy's hands off. "I think this time we should read the instructions."

Dandy nodded. "Good idea."

Malcolm grabbed a small piece of paper out of the box. In bold letters across the top were the words, *WARNING: For Serious Ghost Hunters Only!*

No one was more serious about this than Malcolm. He kept reading.

"What does that mean?" Dandy asked.

Malcolm shrugged. "It just means you have to be a serious ghost hunter."

Dandy rubbed his nose. "Then why don't they just say so?"

"If there's a ghost around, it'll let you know," Malcolm translated.

**❶** When the switch is in the On position, it will heat and activate the necessary sensors. The switch must be on for at least two minutes before detecting. A red light will come on as an indicator.

**❷** Once the sensors are properly heated, the specter detector can then be switched to Detect mode. A blinking gold light and sound pulse will indicate Detect mode. One pulse per second indicates no activity. Three or more pulses per second indicates activity.

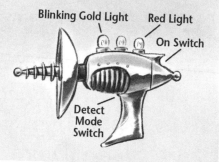

Blinking Gold Light    Red Light

On Switch

Detect Mode Switch

"It has to warm up," Malcolm said.

Dandy looked at Malcolm like a kid lost in a department store. "Huh?"

"It'll make a noise," Malcolm said.

CAUTION: THIS ITEM IS NOT A TOY. PLEASE KEEP AWAY FROM NONPROFESSIONALS.

"We're not professionals," Dandy said.

Malcolm gave him a sour look. "Speak for yourself."

Dandy picked his nose and rubbed his finger on his shirt. "Okay, let's try it out."

"It's not that easy," Malcolm said. "We have to decide where we're going to try it."

"How about right here?" Dandy suggested.

Malcolm laughed out loud. "Here? You think there'd be ghosts around here? Come on, Dandy. The scariest thing around here is Grandma Eunice when she takes her teeth out at night."

"Then where are we going to find ghosts?" Dandy asked.

Malcolm dropped down on his bottom, right in the middle of the floor, and crossed his legs. He was careful to hold the specter detector with both hands. "That's what we have to figure out."

Dandy squatted down next to him and said, "How about the library?"

"Why the library?" Malcolm asked.

"I heard that sometimes the books drop off their shelves by themselves for no reason!"

"Dandy, that rumor was started by Mrs. Crutchmeyer. She's a lonely old librarian who will say anything to get people to come check out books."

Dandy just grunted in agreement. Malcolm suddenly had an idea.

"I've got it!" Malcolm jumped up and hurriedly put the specter detector in a drawer.

"What?" Dandy asked, still sitting.

"The McBleaky house!"

"No!" Dandy shot up off the floor. "No way!"

"Can you think of a better place?" Malcolm argued. "There's no doubt that it's haunted. Everyone knows it."

"And everyone stays away," Dandy added.

"Be a coward, I don't care," Malcolm said. "But I'm going there right now to check it out."

Malcolm headed toward the stairs, then looked back at Dandy. "Are you coming, or would you rather stay here and watch my sister hop around like a kangaroo with the chicken pox?"

Dandy stood for a moment considering. "Let's go," he finally said.

# The Freaky
# McBleaky House

Malcolm and Dandy snuck out the back and raced around to the front. They ran down the sidewalk, their sneakers pounding hard on the hot concrete.

After two blocks, Malcolm decided it was safe to slow down and walk, but he still hurried. He hadn't had this much fun since he invented a windshield wiper for his safety goggles with Cocoa's toothbrush.

The midday traffic hummed as the boys walked toward town. But instead of turning left on Main Street, they turned right and headed uphill, away from the buzz of the community.

Malcolm could see the McBleaky house, standing gray and gloomy up ahead. And the closer they got, the slower they walked, Dandy lagging several steps behind.

"Maybe I should wait here," Dandy said. "I wouldn't want to scare off any of the ghosts."

Malcolm gave him a look. "You couldn't scare a flea off a dog's behind. Keep walking."

Dandy crept slowly behind Malcolm, then shouted, "Wait!"

Malcolm nearly jumped out of his jeans. "Don't give me a heart attack like that! What's wrong?"

"You didn't bring the ghost detector."

Malcolm exhaled a barrel full of nervous air. "I know. We're just scoping the place out right now. Besides it's pointless to try and detect a ghost during the day. Don't you watch horror movies? They only come out at night."

"So when do you plan to look for ghosts?" Dandy asked.

Malcolm grinned. "Tonight."

Dandy turned a sickly shade of white. "A-alone?"

"Don't be silly," Malcolm said. "You're spending the night tonight."

Dandy's face drooped. "Tonight?"

"Don't be such a baby. Let's go."

Malcolm and Dandy walked up to the crumbling picket fence. It was an awesome

sight. Even in the middle of summer, the trees looked dead and mossy. The weeds were taller than the first floor windows, and the second story of the house sagged. The top windows reminded Malcolm of sleepy eyes, waiting and watching.

Malcolm stepped onto the creaky McBleaky porch. He grinned.

"Dandy," he whispered to his jittery friend, "a creaky porch is a definite sign of a haunted house."

A cottony cobweb guarded the front door. "Bingo," Malcolm said. "Another sure sign."

And when he opened the squeaky McBleaky door, he knew he couldn't have picked a better place. Malcolm was sure that nothing was living here. But just as they were about to step in, two hands grabbed their shoulders. Malcolm and Dandy whipped around with a scream.

"Ahhhhhhhhhhh!" A most hideous monster stood inches away!

"I'm going to tell Mom you came here," Cocoa said, pursing her lips.

It took Malcolm a few seconds to catch his breath. "You followed us!"

"That's right," Cocoa said. "I told you I'd pay you back. Now you're in big trouble, mister."

"Well, if I'm in trouble then so are you. You're here too." Malcolm gave Cocoa a smug grin.

"Not if I tell Mom that I followed you because I knew you were up to something," Cocoa said.

"And I'll tell Mom that you don't mind your own business," Malcolm argued.

Cocoa pressed her fists to her hips. "I'll tell Mom that you could have been killed out here, and I was only doing it for your own good."

"I'll tell Mom that I saw you kissing Carson O'Donnell behind the school last week."

Cocoa gasped and covered her mouth. "You didn't see that," she whispered.

"Yes, I did," Malcolm said. "And you're just lucky I haven't told Mom before now."

Cocoa stood up tall and raised her nose in the air. "Fine. I won't say anything if you won't."

"Fine," Malcolm said. "Now go away."

Cocoa stepped off the rickety porch and pushed through the tall weeds. She looked back and yelled, "But you better bring back my blow-dryer!"

Once she was gone, Dandy shook his head. "Your sister is weird."

Malcolm nodded. "But not as weird as this old house. It's perfect. We're definitely coming back tonight."

# Granny-Sitting

Malcolm sat with his family at dinner that evening, but his mind was on ghost detecting. Everyone was unusually quiet. Dad had the TV blaring from the living room so he could hear the six o'clock news. Malcolm saw his chance to launch Step One of his ghost-hunting plan.

"Mom, can Dandy spend the night?"

"Of course," Mom said. "He can keep you company while you watch Grandma Eunice."

The spaghetti in Malcolm's mouth suddenly tasted like lead. "I'm watching Grandma Eunice tonight?"

"It's just for a few hours," Mom said.

"Why can't Cocoa watch her?"

Mom laid down her fork. "Because Cocoa is going with me."

"Why can't I go?" Malcolm asked. He didn't really want to go anywhere with them, but he wanted to protest.

Mom sighed and lifted her fork again. "You can go if you think you'll enjoy shopping for Cocoa's new dress."

Cocoa wrinkled her nose and smirked at him.

Malcolm wouldn't give up. "Why can't Dad watch Grandma?"

"Bowling night," Dad said, shoveling spaghetti into his mouth.

Malcolm sank in his chair. It was useless. He looked over at Grandma Eunice, who didn't seem to notice they were talking about her. She had a large napkin tucked in her collar, and there appeared to be more spaghetti on her chin and fingers than on her plate.

He spoke to her in a defeated voice. "I'm staying with you tonight, Grandma Eunice."

She gave him a tomatoey grin. "That's nice."

His plan to sneak back to the McBleaky house might not work after all.

That evening, Grandma Eunice sat on the edge of the sofa,

watching an old black-and-white TV show. Dandy was lying on the floor, using Cocoa's blow-dryer to balance a ping-pong ball. The ball floated on the steady jet of warm air—a trick Malcolm had shown him a few weeks ago.

Malcolm was stretched out on the other end of the couch, tapping the toes of his sneakers together out of pure boredom. He looked at his watch. Eight thirty. What time

did the mall close, anyway?  Knowing Mom and Cocoa, they'd stop off for a soda or ice cream afterward.  And Dad wouldn't be home until after eleven o'clock.

Dandy shut off the blow-dryer and let the ping-pong ball drop.  It dribbled across the floor, then rolled into the corner.  "When can we go?" he asked.

Malcolm sat up.  "We may not be able to go at all tonight.  I don't think I can sneak out if it's very late."

Grandma Eunice threw her head back and laughed at something on TV.

"Maybe we shouldn't be talking about this in front of your great-grandmother," Dandy whispered, pointing her way.

"It's okay," Malcolm said.  "She doesn't know what's going on."

"Oh well," Dandy said.  "I don't want to

go to that house at night anyway. That place was scary enough in the daylight."

"I just have to go," Malcolm said. "And I'm taking my camera. If my specter detector can really detect a ghost, I might be able to capture it on film."

Grandma Eunice laughed again, this time slapping her leg. A bit of drool rolled down the corner of her face.

"Maybe there's another house we could test it out on," Dandy suggested.

Malcolm shook his head furiously. "No, it has to be the McBleaky house!"

Suddenly the television shut off. Malcolm looked over at Grandma Eunice. She sat with the remote still extended in her hand. Her face looked young and bright, and her eyes were lit like someone half her age. "You don't want to go there," she said.

Malcolm leaned toward her and looked her in the eyes. "Grandma?"

"You don't want to go to the McBleaky house," Grandma Eunice warned. "It's not fit for any living soul, especially little boys."

Malcolm couldn't believe it. His great-grandmother had some wits about her after all. "How do you know about the McBleaky house?" he asked, still not convinced she was totally all there.

"Because I knew Old Man McBleaky himself. And I know what happened in that house."

"What?" Malcolm and Dandy asked, huddling together.

Grandma Eunice moved in closer to the boys. "It all started about 80 years ago . . ."

# The Tale

Malcolm and Dandy leaned toward Grandma Eunice. Her eyes looked distant. Not like before when she was in another world, but like she was remembering.

She continued, "The McBleakys built that house in the 1920s. They had two boys, Howard and Herbert. Howard was the serious one, always worried about school and his paper route. Herbert was the joker. He made Howard's life miserable, constantly putting dead flies in his ice cubes or fishing

string across the bottom of his doorway. Howard hated it. He swore he'd get Herbert back one day.

"Their parents were killed when they were young men. Their mother was struck by lightning while hanging out the wash, and their dad caught it in a tractor accident. Both within just a couple of months of each other.

"The boys were left alone in that house, but they were old enough to look after themselves. Everyone thought that with the parents gone Herbert would straighten up and get serious. No sir. He kept right on pulling those awful jokes on his brother.

"But then Herbert up and kicked the bucket himself. No one ever knew the true cause of his death. But Neb Fuller, the barber, overheard Howard whispering at the funeral, 'Guess I got the last laugh.'

"Within a few days, Howard started

coming into town, his eyes all red and bloodshot, his face weary and tired. 'What's wrong, Howard?' people would ask. He'd just lift his heavy head and say, 'Can't sleep.'

"Then he started aging real fast. He became bitter and frail. He'd hobble around town shaking his fist and hollering at folks. People stayed out of his way.

"One day, I saw a crowd by the fence of the McBleaky house. An ambulance was parked in front, and two men in white coats were hauling Howard out the door. He was dressed in nothing but his boxer shorts. He was screaming at the top of his lungs, 'I can't take it anymore! He's still playing tricks on me!' It was a pitiful sight.

"After that, no one's been able to stay in that house. Not one living soul. Herbert's ghost is still there, and he's as loony as ever. So I suggest you and your friend here find another place to try out your ghost gadget."

Malcolm blinked. Was he dreaming?

"Grandma Eunice, I can't believe it. You still have all your marbles!"

"Yes, sir," she said, tapping a crooked finger to her head. "They're all right here."

"Then why are you always pretending to be on Planet Weird?"

Grandma Eunice laughed. "I act the way I'm treated. I tried to convince your mother a long time ago that I'm sane. But for some reason, she and everyone else wants to treat me like I'm one banana short of a bunch. I just go along with it to make them happy. Besides, it keeps me from having to take a turn doing the dishes."

Malcolm couldn't resist. He reached over and gave Grandma Eunice a hug.

"Now," she said, "why don't you and Alfred here go on to your laboratory and find something fun to do? I'm okay."

Malcolm and Dandy hopped up and headed out of the room.

"And Malcolm, honey," Grandma Eunice called out, "try not to talk about me while I'm in the room."

When he looked back, she winked and smiled.

# Sneaking Out—Sneaking In

Grandma Eunice's story was meant as a warning. But, it just confirmed what Malcolm already knew. The McBleaky house was definitely haunted!

Malcolm's luck was running high. His mom and sister came home early, and Mom went straight to bed, complaining of a headache.

The two boys took their sleeping bags to the basement, claiming they'd sleep down in the lab. Malcolm locked the basement

door and pulled out a backpack he'd packed that afternoon.

"What's in there?" Dandy asked.

"Everything we'll need to detect a ghost," Malcolm answered.

"Don't we just need the specter detector?"

Malcolm rolled his eyes. "And a flashlight and a tape recorder and a camera."

"What about a snack?"

"Dandy, honestly, why would we need a snack?"

"In case we get hungry."

Malcolm couldn't believe it. Dandy was serious. "We're not going to get hungry. We won't be there long enough to get hungry! And if you happen to get hungry, maybe the ghost will be polite and offer you something to eat."

Dandy shrugged. "Okay."

Malcolm opened the skinny basement window, climbed up on a chair and slithered out. He looked back in at Dandy. "You're not going to chicken out, are you?"

Dandy hopped up on the chair. "I'm right behind you."

And Dandy stayed right behind Malcolm the whole way. About three feet back, dragging the soles of his sneakers and biting his fingernails.

Malcolm had the jitters, too. Partly from fear, partly from excitement. He had to be brave. This was his one shot at fame. If he could detect a ghost, record it, and capture it on film, he'd be written up in every major newspaper in the country . . . make that in the world! He wished he'd brought the video camera.

The McBleaky house stood just ahead of

them, like a black hole ready to suck them in. Malcolm could hear Dandy's teeth chattering. Once they were hidden by the towering weeds, Malcolm pulled out the flashlight and clicked it on. A circle of white light hit the porch, and Malcolm saw an army of tiny critters skittering into the shadows.

Dandy gulped loudly when they reached the door. "Are you sure we should go in there? That's trespassing."

"Who would come and arrest us?" Malcolm asked. "Even the cops are afraid of this place."

Dandy grabbed Malcolm's shoulder. "Shouldn't that tell you something? If cops are afraid, then what are a couple of dumb kids like us doing here?"

Malcolm set the backpack down and pulled out his specter detector. "This," he said with pride. "Now, do as I say, and don't be a baby."

The door opened easily. *Eeeeeeeek.*

Malcolm stepped in, turned on the specter detector, then pointed the flashlight at his watch. "It's warming up."

Dandy still had a death grip on Malcolm's shoulder. "I have to use the bathroom."

"No, you don't," Malcolm said, not taking his eyes off his watch. "Two minutes, that's all it'll take."

The house was still and quiet. The only noises were the ticking of Malcolm's watch and Dandy's ragged breathing. They waited. *Tick. Tick. Tick.*

Something moved in the corner. Malcolm whipped the flashlight around and stabbed

the darkness. A mouse scurried across and disappeared into a crack.

Only one minute. He counted the seconds silently, *one Frankenstein, two Frankenstein, three Frankenstein.* Dandy's grip had become a serious squeeze, but in less than a minute they'd be on the move.

When the second hand hit the two minute mark, Malcolm reached for the switch. "You ready?" he asked Dandy.

Dandy stood paralyzed. Malcolm figured he wasn't going to get an answer, and flipped the specter detector to Detect. The green light flashed off, and the gold light flashed on. But only for a second. The light then blinked off and on with a steady *bleep—bleep—bleep.*

"Not much activity right now," Malcolm said, turning to look back at Dandy. Dandy's eyes were wide-open. His lips

looked blue, even in the brassy hue of the flicking specter detector light.

"Just stick with me," Malcolm said, although he figured Dandy wasn't thinking for a second of venturing off on his own. Malcolm took slow baby steps, tiptoeing across the floor, Dandy's hand still gripping him. Dandy never lifted his feet. He skated behind Malcolm, without a breath.

Malcolm kept the flashlight pointed in his left hand, the detector in his right. As they approached the fireplace, two eyes peered down at them.

"What?" Malcolm sputtered, whipping the light toward the mantle. Just an ugly giant moose head, hung up like a trophy. Malcolm took a moment to breathe and gather everything that was just scared out of him.

When they reached a spiral staircase, Malcolm whispered to Dandy, "Reach in my

backpack and turn on the tape recorder. Then pull out the camera and turn on the flash."

Dandy never said a word. He obeyed Malcolm, but took forever doing it because of his nervous fumbling. And even though Malcolm tried to stand still, the light from the flashlight danced all over the foot of the staircase. But Malcolm was patient. He had to be. He hadn't told Dandy, but he'd stay here all night if he had to.

As it turned out, he didn't have to wait long. Like a fisherman hoping for a catch, Malcolm had a bite. The gold light blinked faster.

*Bleep-bleep-bleep-bleep-bleep.*

Both boys froze, staring down at the rapid signal. The beam from the flashlight bent and flickered. Then something brushed the hairs on Malcolm's neck. A voice, as thin as the wind, whispered in Malcolm's ear.

"It creeeeeeeps."

# It Creeps!

Malcolm's guts turned to jelly. Fear spread through him, tingling from head to toe. The specter detector kept on detecting.

*Bleep-bleep-bleep-bleep-bleep.*

Malcolm turned to see Dandy standing like a zombie. His lips were purple and his eyes hollow.

"Run, Dandy!" Malcolm screamed. He turned and ran for the front door. He tugged and tugged, but the door was bolted shut.

Malcolm slumped against the door. He had to think . . . he had to plan . . . he had to decide what to do next. He'd been so preoccupied with detecting a ghost, he never stopped to think about what he'd do when he found one.

The specter detector sped up. *Bleep-bleep-bleep-bleep-bleep-bleep!*

The kitchen door was just across the room. If he could make it there, he could blast through and rush out the back. But as he darted toward it, something caught his hair and jerked him back. He landed splat on his bottom. The flashlight crashed to the floor and everything went black.

"It creeeeeeeeps. It creeeeeeeeps."

"Yeow!" Malcolm came off the floor faster than a cat on hot sand. He sprinted toward the kitchen, bumping into Dandy, who still stood petrified. Just as Malcolm

reached the kitchen door, it swung open, but before he entered, it slammed shut again . . . smashing him right in the face.

He staggered backward, stars falling in front of his face. The dark room went in and out of focus. But Malcolm could still hear the specter detector beeping away, even faster now.

*Bleep-bleep-bleep-bleep-bleep-bleep-bleep-bleep!* In his daze, he heard that wispy voice. "It creeeeeeeeps. It creeeeeeeeps."

He fell into the kitchen and looked around. No back door! Was this a joke? He crawled under a large rusty sink. He had to collect his thoughts, or at least the ones that hadn't been whacked out of him by the kitchen door.

He took a deep breath. *Think! Think!* Now his specter detector bleeped faster than a baseball card on bicycle spokes.

*Bleepbleepbleepbleepbleepbleepbleepbleepbleep!* Something grabbed Malcolm's nose, tweaking it hard. "It creeeeeeeps. It creeeeeeeps."

"Ouch!" Malcolm shot out from behind the sink and pushed through the kitchen door again. "Dandy!" he screamed. Dandy just stood there, not even blinking.

Malcolm hid under the stairs. It was just an inky black hole, with the exception of the gold light from the specter detector, now bleeping so fast, it generated one continuous beam. *Bleeeeeeeeeeeeeeeeeeeeeeeeeep!* Malcolm knew what that meant.

"It creeeeeeeps. It creeeeeeeps."

He jumped out from under the stairs and tried to run, but someone or something had knotted his shoelaces. He tripped and fell forward. The specter detector dropped from his hands and skittered across the floor.

Malcolm crawled on his elbows and belly, slithering like a snake. In a panic, he grabbed the gadget and tried flipping the switch off. It was jammed.

*Bleeeeeeeeeeeeeeeeeeeeeeeeeep!*

He jiggled it and tugged at it.

*Bleeeeeeeeeeeeeeeeeeeeeeeeeep!*

He banged it on the floor.

*Bleeeeeeeeeeeeeeeeeeeeeeeeeep!*

Then in a moment of desperation, he opened the little door and popped out the batteries.

*Bleeeeeeeeeeeeeeeeeeeeeeeeeep!*

Malcolm stared wildly at the specter detector. Was he losing his mind?

*Bleeeeeeeeeeeeeeeeeeeeeeeeeep!*

"It creeeeeeeeps. It creeeeeeeeps."

Malcolm hung his head and whimpered. He didn't need his specter detector. What he had come to find had found him.

"It creeeeeeeeps. It creeeeeeeeps."

Malcolm couldn't take it anymore. "What creeps! What creeps!"

"YOUR UNDERWEAR!"

Suddenly something lifted Malcolm in the air by the elastic waistband of his drawers. Yanked higher and higher. He thought he'd split in two. Then it hooked him on one pointed antler of the moose head over the fireplace. And there Malcolm hung, like a wet sock.

The specter detector went silent. The light dimmed and disappeared. And just as Malcolm's breathing slowed, a brilliant flash filled the room. A giant spot appeared before his eyes.

"What was that?" he yelled.

Dandy flipped on the flashlight and aimed it at Malcolm's face. "Didn't you want me to take a picture?"

# Winding Down

"How'd you get up there?" Dandy asked.

Malcolm shook his head. "You didn't see? You didn't hear?"

Dandy shrugged, then he looked around until he found an old broom to help get Malcolm loose from the moose.

Malcolm couldn't believe his underwear could stretch that far! He wondered if any was left covering his behind. With the help

of the broom handle, he managed to pluck the elastic free and fall to the ground.

"Let's go!" he yelled.

After the boys snatched up their things, including the specter detector, Dandy ran for the front door.

"It's locked," Malcolm said. "We'll have to find another exit." But Dandy turned the handle and the door opened with a gentle squeak.

Wasting no time, they raced out the door, scampered over the rickety porch, trudged through the weedy walkway, and jumped the wobbly picket fence. They didn't stop until they reached Malcolm's front yard, where they collapsed on the lawn, gasping and groaning.

"What were we running away from?" Dandy asked.

Malcolm buried his face in this hands. "I can't believe you didn't see it or hear it."

"I saw the light on the ghost detector blinking," Dandy said. "It blinked and blinked and blinked . . ." Dandy's eyelids relaxed and he stared off in a trance.

"It must have hypnotized you!" Malcolm said. He snapped his fingers in front of Dandy's eyes to wake him up.

"Anyway," Dandy continued, "the next thing I knew, you were hanging from that moose."

Malcolm stood up and looked at his bottom. The elastic of his underwear was drooping over his pants. "Let's go in," he said.

Dandy stared off down the street. "All this ghost hunting has made me tired. I think I'll go home."

Malcolm watched as Dandy drifted down the sidewalk like someone sleepwalking. He disappeared around the corner.

Malcolm still had the jitters when he slipped into his house. Even though Dandy had gone, he still had the feeling he wasn't alone. He was being watched. Had someone or something followed him home?

He moved quietly to his lab to put away his equipment. As he reached the basement door, he met with another shock. Cocoa was blocking the way, hands on her hips, and her mouth tight as a wire.

"Where is it?" she growled.

"What?"

"Where is my blow-dryer?"

Malcolm's shoulders sank. He was in no mood to deal with her tonight. "I'll get it in the morning," he said.

"Look at my hair! It looks like a heap of spaghetti. I need my blow-dryer! Get it tonight!"

She screamed so hard that Malcolm could see clear down her throat. "Okay, okay," he said. "I'll put it in your bathroom."

Cocoa stormed away, slamming her bedroom door.

The excitement of the evening wore off, and Malcolm's feet suddenly felt like bricks. He trudged down the stairs and put his equipment away. He found Cocoa's blow-dryer where Dandy had hidden it. He looked at it for a moment, then pulled out his specter detector.

*Hmmmmm*... An evil thought crossed his mind. Herbert McBleaky wasn't the only practical joker in town. He slipped in and out of Cocoa's bathroom with a devilish grin.

# Payback

Malcolm had a night full of weird dreams where he was chased by ghosts, his sister, and a large moose. He could barely tell one from the other. But the sun, shining on his face, told him it was time to get up and start the day.

He sat down to his usual bowl of cereal. Everything seemed unusually white and transparent this morning. Malcolm figured it was just a trick of the light.

Mom stood at the stove, making eggs for Dad. Dad sat at the end of the table, reading the newspaper. And Grandma Eunice sat eating her prunes. It appeared to be a normal summer morning.

Grandma looked shriveled and small staring at the back of the newspaper. Then Malcolm noticed the light in her eyes. She wasn't staring off . . . she was reading the article! She turned to Malcolm and winked, then went back to her reading. Malcolm couldn't help but smile.

Malcolm poured his milk and dug into his breakfast. Before he got the spoon to his mouth, a bloodcurdling scream echoed down the hall from the bathroom.

Dad spilled his coffee. Mom dropped a plate. Grandma Eunice dribbled prune juice down her chin. And a moment later, Cocoa came rushing through the kitchen holding

the specter detector, her wet hair slapping against her face as she ran past the table.

Malcolm couldn't see what was chasing her, but he was pretty sure it was the ghost that had followed him home last night.

Cocoa raced about, jumping and grabbing her bottom like someone was popping her with a towel.

Mom and Dad ran after her. Malcolm just sat and ate his cereal. He guessed that the specter detector would fix Cocoa's spaghetti hair problem. After this, it should be standing straight up!

Payback was fun, but there was more work to do.

Malcolm got dressed, then hurried down the street to the nearest mailbox. It was time to send off for another weird gadget. *The Ecto-Handheld-Automatic-Heat-Sensitive-Laser-Enhanced Ghost Zapper. Guaranteed to zap the peskiest of ghosts. *Batteries not included.*

# TOP FIVE WAYS TO DETECT A GHOST, SPIRIT, OR POLTERGEIST

*From Ghost Detectors Malcolm and Dandy*

1. Check for creepy surroundings. Is there a graveyard nearby? Or an area covered in strange shadows? Is there a house that stares at you?

2. Ask people if there are stories about the area. Is there a legend about a haunting? Has anyone else seen a spirit there?

3. Listen to the area at night. Do you hear moaning, whispering, or laughter that doesn't belong?

4. Cautiously enter the area. Does the porch creak? Are there cobwebs all around?

5. Turn on your specter detector and wait for the *bleep*. Just be sure to keep close to the wall and try not to trip on your shoelaces! You never know what will be around the next corner!